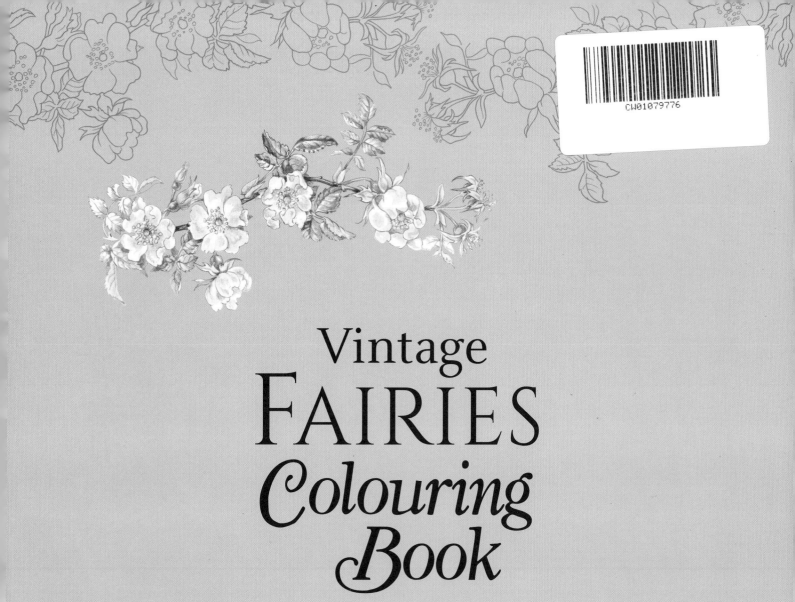

Vintage
FAIRIES
Colouring
Book

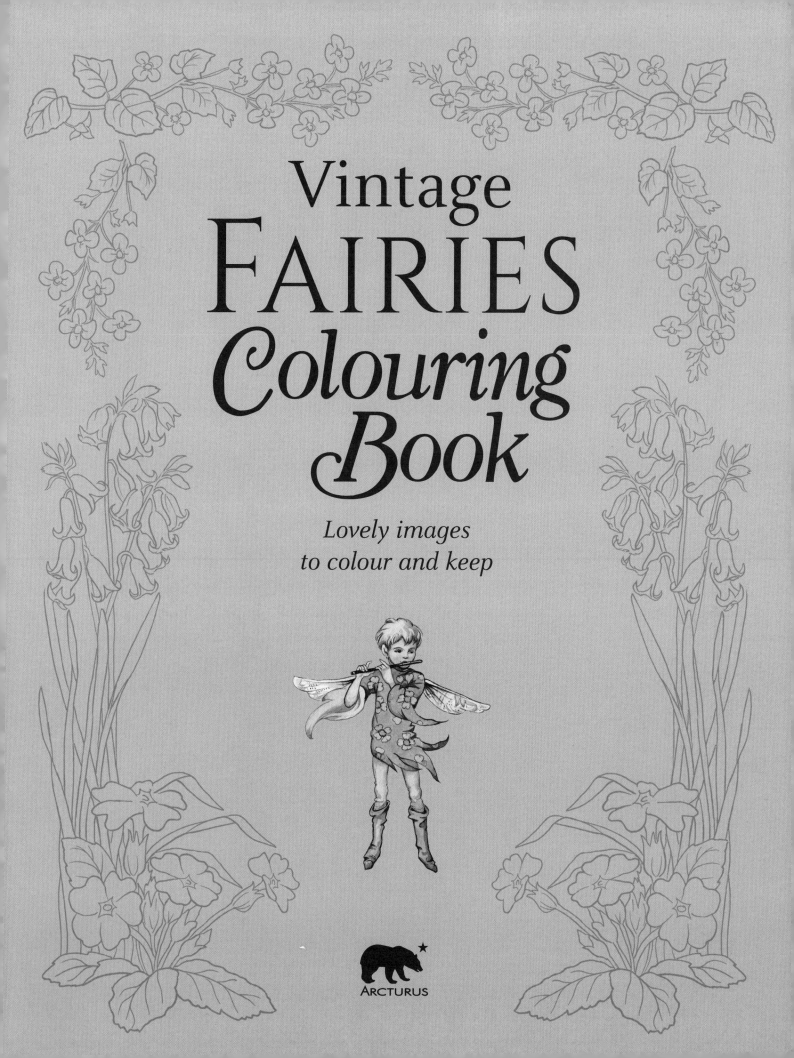

Vintage
FAIRIES
Colouring
Book

*Lovely images
to colour and keep*

ARCTURUS

ARCTURUS

This edition published in 2019 by Arcturus Publishing Limited
26/27 Bickels Yard, 151–153 Bermondsey Street,
London SE1 3HA

Copyright © Arcturus Holdings Limited

ISBN: 978-1-78888-775-5
CH006920NT
Supplier 29, Date 1218, Print run 8063

All images courtesy of the Medici Society/Mary Evans Picture Library

Printed in China

Created for children 10+

Introduction

The early 20th century was an era of uncertainty, riven by war and shaken by the rapid pace of technological change. The artists whose work is included in this book seemed to yearn for a simpler, more innocent time, which they evoked in illustrations of idyllic, pastoral landscapes populated by winsome fairy folk.

The French Symbolist artist Gustave Moreau said: 'I believe only in what I do not see', and the illustrations in this book bear out his maxim. Including recognizable features of everyday life transmuted into an elfin dimension – a toadstool carousel, a butterfly postman, a honeysuckle blossom serving as an ear trumpet – the delightful, detailed tableaux are rendered with great skill and charm.

Each image has a corresponding black-and-white line drawing, which you can work on either by using the artist's original colour scheme or your own choice of shades.

RENE
CLOKE